Help Wanted:

Wednesdays Only

Help Wanted:
Wednesdays Only

by Peggy Dymond Leavey

Napoleon Publishing

Cover illustration by Greg Ruhl

Book design by Pamela Kinney
Cover design by Pamela Kinney

Published by Napoleon Publishing Inc.
Toronto, Ontario, Canada

05 04 03 02 01 00 99 98   5 4 3 2

Printed in Canada

Canadian Cataloguing in Publication Data

> Leavey, Peggy Dymond
> Help wanted : Wednesdays only

> ISBN 0-929141-23-7

> I. Title

> PS8573. E38H4 1994 jC813' .54 C94-931073-5
> PZ7.L43He 1994

For Dad.
H. G. P. D.
1906 - 1992

CHAPTER 1

"Whoa, Mark! Isn't that your grandfather?" A black and white police cruiser was parked at the curb outside my building. Jason bent down for a closer look.

At first, the glass in the window only reflected our two bewildered faces, pale and pinched from the bitter March wind. Then my heart sank. It *was* Grandpa. How could he do this to me? Again.

"Mark Rogers?" One of the officers got out of the car onto the sidewalk.

"Look, Mark," gulped Jason, "I gotta go. Okay? I'll call you later." And he scurried away up the street.

It wasn't that Jason was a chicken or anything like that. He just knew how to stay out of unpleasant situations. I was glad it had only been Jason with me. He already knew about my grandfather. I was glad it hadn't been Nicole or someone else I was trying to impress. Not that

Nicole Somers would be walking home with a shrimpy kid like me anyway. But I sure didn't want any of the kids at school to see my grandfather getting out of a police car. In his pyjamas.

I could feel my face burning with shame as I led the officers up to our apartment.

"Must've walked all the way over here from his place," one of them said, waiting while I unlocked the door. "Found him wandering around about three blocks away."

"Have your mother call us," the other officer directed, seeing us both safely inside.

I closed the door and stood leaning against it, looking at my grandfather. I had never used to feel pity for this man who sat here now on the couch, his thin, brown hands resting on his knees. Once he had been my hero.

I'll look like that someday, I thought. Everyone said I took after Luigi Cecchini, except he had thick black hair and mine was red, like my father's. Grandpa and I had the same wiry body, not very tall, but strong as an ox, they said. At least, he had been once. I'd seen him lift a crate of cabbages onto his shoulders as if they had been feathers.

Mom had given him those pyjamas for Christmas. There was a little blue snowflake

8

design on the white flannelette. Like a little kid's.

"How come you didn't get dressed today, Grandpa?" I asked.

"I get dressed, Frankie. I always get dressed."

"But where's your coat? It's freezing outside."

Frankie was my mother's brother. He'd been killed in a motorcycle accident before I was even born.

"Mom will be home at five," I sighed. "You want to watch T.V.?"

On the screen, some talk show host was raving at his studio audience, and Grandpa, although he never moved back from the edge of the couch, looked as though he might watch it for a few minutes. You could never be sure. He was pretty restless these days.

I went into the kitchen to see what I could find to eat. I was 13 at the time, old enough to know what was happening to my grandfather, but I still didn't really understand it.

* * *

That was Wednesday. On Thursday, Mrs. Fuller, the woman who looked after Grandpa during the day, (when he wasn't escaping), dropped by to talk to Mom.

Jason and I were spread out on the floor of the living room, trying to think up something to do for our science project. So far, all we had was a big sheet of white poster board, as blank as our brains.

Jason Thomas and I were pretty close. The third one in our little group of friends who hung around together was Travis Devries. He had to do his science project with another partner this time. Only two could work together, the teacher had said.

Travis had gotten teamed up with Nicole and he didn't mind a bit. He'd probably get straight 'A's'. I wouldn't have minded working with Nicole either. Except I didn't want her to find out that science was far from my best subject.

"I think it has reached a point where your father should not be alone at night anymore, Giovanna," Mrs Fuller was saying. An island counter was all that divided the kitchen from the living room in our apartment, so no conversation was ever private.

Mom hacked at the hamburger in the frying pan. "I'm at my wits' end about this," she said. "I can't afford to have anyone stay with him nights. And there's no room for him here. You can see the size of this place."

I picked up the felt marker and wrote,

10

"Science Project. Jason Thomas and Mark Rogers," along a line I'd drawn at the top of the poster.

"Now what?" asked Jason, pushing his glasses back up the ridge of his nose and squinting at me expectantly. "Everyone else will have the same old rock collection or models of the solar system. Can't we come up with something different?"

"I've given it a lot of thought since we talked to the doctor the last time," we heard Mom saying, "and I think the only solution is for us to move in with him."

My mouth and Jason's fell open at the same instant. Except mine was making a sound like choking. The marker dropped onto the paper, leaving a black splotch in the middle of the poster. I scrambled to my feet.

"I haven't had a minute yet to discuss this with my son," my mother admitted to Mrs. Fuller.

"Mark!" hissed Jason, yanking on the leg of my jeans. "Is it true?"

"No way," I growled. Mom was holding the door open for her visitor and she put up her hand to warn me to back off.

"We'll discuss it later, Mark. Okay?" she said. I could hardly believe what I'd heard. She had to be kidding!

"I'd better be going too," said Jason,

abandoning the project on the floor and coming around to the door. "I'll see you later, Mark."

"Chili, Jason. Remember?" said Mom.

"That's okay, Mrs. Rogers." Jason grabbed his jacket off the back of the chair. "I gotta check in at home. Besides," he shot me a quick look, "you guys probably want to talk."

"I can tell the idea upsets you, Mark," said Mom, when the door had shut on the back of my fleeing friend.

"Well, good. Because I know I didn't hear you right. You're not really thinking of moving to Grandpa's?"

She put the plates on the table, the silverware on top, waiting for me to set it all straight. We usually did this together while I told her about my day at school. Now I sat down and waited for her explanation. Mom sat down too and faced me.

"Do you have any other solution?" she asked. "I mean it. If you have any ideas, I'd really like to hear them."

I had to come up with an alternate plan to this blockbuster idea of hers. After all, this was something that would affect my whole life. I hadn't thought we were going to have to make any decisions about Grandpa so soon. He had been getting worse, more muddled and forgetful, but it had been happening gradually. Now here was Mom springing this plan on me right out of the blue.

"You were the one who told me something had to be done when your grandfather showed up here in his pyjamas again the other day," Mom went on.

"I know. But not this. Not us having to go and live with him!"

"We're the only family he has, Mark. If not us, who else?"

"How much would it cost anyway, to have someone stay with him at night? Someone like Mrs. Fuller."

"Too much, let me tell you." She scraped chili out onto my plate, but I just pushed the beans around on it, not feeling much like eating. Jason's favourite meal. We ate it a lot at our place because it was fast and cheap.

"You can't expect me to move away over there. This is where all my friends are."

"You make friends easily, Mark." Mom set the plastic bag with the bread in it on the table and sat down herself. "Your grandfather's house is small, I know, but it's big enough for three."

"Make that two. Because I'm not going."

Mom didn't say anything for a while and we both kept our eyes on our plates. Somebody had to have a better idea than this. My mind was churning.

"Well, what about school?" I demanded. I knew how much my education meant to my

13

mother. "I'd have to change schools. Again. That can't be good."

"I know, and it won't be easy for you, either. I'd really like to be able to hang on until you graduate, but this disease of Grandpa's won't wait."

Alzheimer's. I knew all about it, and that there was no cure. I just hadn't thought it was going to affect me.

Mom put her hand over mine; I drew back quickly to reach for a slice of bread that I really didn't want.

"Try to see the bind I'm in, Mark," she begged. "Please."

"What about me? Is anyone thinking about me?"

"Of course I am. But you're young, Mark. You'll adjust."

This wasn't one bit fair. Just because I was young. In the past two years I'd done just about all the adjusting anyone should be expected to do. It had been bad enough moving here, leaving behind everything I'd grown up with. Even my dog.

Mom must have been reading my thoughts. "Maybe you could have another dog, Mark. Your grandfather's got a little back yard." I recognize bribery when I hear it.

In our other place, before Dad left, I'd had a dog. But there were no pets allowed in this apartment, so when Mom and I had moved here, I'd left Chelsea behind with my best friend, David.

Leaving Chelsea had been the worst part about moving two years ago. I knew, even though I was just a little kid, that Mom was hurting over the separation, and I was feeling mad at my dad. I'd have gone anywhere if I'd thought it could make my mom happy.

But things were different now. Mom liked her work, I had Jason and Travis to hang around with, and I had my own after-school job. I was even on better terms with Dad, 'though I didn't see much of him now that he'd moved away from the city.

I couldn't ever have Chelsea back. She'd been hit by a car last summer, and when David called to tell me, I hadn't even recognized my old friend's voice.

I went to bed feeling mean inside about Grandpa. It didn't feel good. Why did things have to be this way? My great-grandfather on my father's side was 90 and still driving his own car. And my Grandma Joyce, my father's mother, had started university after she was 65.

It didn't seem so long ago that my Grandpa Luigi had been just as normal as everyone else. It had started with his being a little forgetful. Now he couldn't remember if he'd

15

already done something simple. Like getting dressed. We found him wearing two pairs of pants one day. He'd forgotten he'd put on the underneath pair.

It had been kind of funny at first. Mom stuck little reminders around his house for a while, so that Grandpa'd know to turn off the stove and put things back in the fridge. The worst part was when he'd cry. That's what he did sometimes when he didn't get things right. I think inside his head he knew what he wanted to say, but sometimes the words came out all wrong. That was my theory, anyway. I was glad my grandmother couldn't see the way her Luigi was now.

Grandpa had run a fruit and vegetable business in this city until he retired. For years, he'd left his house before the sun was up. Every morning, he'd gone downtown to the big market to buy produce from the growers who trucked it in from outside the city.

Then he'd gone back to his store in time to open up. Every day the same thing, long hard hours of work, but he usedto say he could never do anything else. Back home in Italy, his ancestors had run the same type of business.

It seemed like hours that I tossed from one side to the other that night, the bed sheets underneath me getting twisted and digging tracks into my back. I knew that, although my grandfather didn't act much like the person I used to love to visit when my grandmother was alive, he was the same person underneath. That was what Alzheimer's disease did.

* * *

In the morning, I could tell by the worn look on her face that Mom hadn't slept well either. The phone rang and she talked softly to someone on the other end. When she hung up she told me that a friend of hers had agreed to take over our apartment if we decided to go. "That would let us out of the lease, Mark." As if that were the only problem.

But before she left for work, I gave in. What else could I do? "Look, Mom, if there's no other way to look after Grandpa, then I guess we should move to his place." There, I'd said it.

"Oh, Mark. Thank you." She put her arms around me and gave me a tight hug. "I know it's a sacrifice you're making. I'm so proud of you." She dabbed at her eyes and tucked the tissue into her purse.

I felt a little like a hypocrite. It wasn't all sacrifice. I was sparing myself the humiliation of having my grandfather show up here again in his pyjamas. Or worse.

My friends were waiting for me outside the school when I got off the bus. Jason had already told Travis about what had been happening at our place last night.

"So? What did you decide?" they both wanted to know.

"We're going, I guess."

"Jeez, Mark. That's a rip-off!" Travis declared.

"Naw. Not really. My grandfather's too sick now to live alone."

"So you guys have to move? Why don't you just put him in a nursing home? My great-grandmother's in one. It's not so bad."

"Mom thinks that's what'll happen when he gets too sick for us to look after," I said.

Jason must have been remembering the times we'd visited my grandfather's together. "That would be too bad," he said. "Remember the time he took us to the carnival after we'd helped him close the store for the night? Remember all the stuff we won? Could he ever throw those darts!"

I swung my book bag over my shoulder, remembering too. "Well, Mom and I are going to see that he stays in his own house just as long as he can."

"Too much!" said Travis, and the bell rang for us to go inside.

* * *

On Saturday, Mom and I went over to see what Grandpa thought about all this. She told me that change in routine sometimes upsets people with Alzheimer's. So we were going to have to approach the subject slowly, just let him get used to the idea.

We found Grandpa puttering around in the tool shed at the back of his place.

"Are you busy, Dad?" Mom asked. He seemed surprised to see us, although we came over every weekend.

"I look for piece of chain," he said. "To fasten that gate. Those chickens they going to get out if I don't find it." He was rummaging through a basket filled with bits of wire and pipe and stiffened paint brushes.

"Can you come in the house a minute, Dad? I'll make us some lunch. Mark and I want to talk to you."

"I ate already," said Grandpa, but he followed us anyway, keeping a hand on my shoulder and letting Mom lead the way up the broken sidewalk to the kitchen door.

There weren't any chickens around here for miles, except in my grandfather's imagination. But then, you never knew in this neighbourhood. Mrs. Salud down the street kept a goat.

Grandpa lived in what everyone called "the

19

East End." In this part of the city, the houses were older and smaller and closer together than in other neighbourhoods, and everyone spoke with a different accent. In the summertime, the people here grew all sorts of weird stuff in their little yards, strange vegetables which crawled up and over the fences, squashes and melons the size of basketballs. And in the front of the houses, where you'd expect grass to be growing, tomato and potato plants often replaced green lawns.

Grandpa had no objections to Mom's plans, but I'm not sure he understood what was happening.

"We'll try not to make too many changes too quickly, Mark," Mom decided, as we rocked together gently on the streetcar ride back home that night.

I told her even Grandpa was bound to notice he had two extra people living in the house. That made her laugh and we both felt better. But maybe we'd have to wait a bit before we introduced the idea of a dog in the family.

CHAPTER 2

It was Easter weekend when Mom and I moved our stuff across the city to Grandpa's. On Sunday, Jason and his mother brought over some of the smaller boxes from our place and Jason stayed on to visit. Together, we checked out the neighbourhood. It wasn't something you could do on your own. People would stare at a kid walking up and down the street by himself. This wasn't a new neighbourhood to me, but I was looking at it now as someone who was going to have to live here.

Back at home, Travis and Nicole were making a working model of a volcano for their science project. They'd probably win. They deserved to; they'd worked together on it every night for two weeks. I guess Nicole wasn't going to miss me after all. I never did anything to let her know I'd hoped she'd be my girlfriend.

I knew a lot of Grandpa's older neighbours already. More than once someone stopped Jason and me on the street. "Hey, kid. How's Luigi doing?" they wanted to know.

The shops on what passed for the main street in this part of the city were small and run down. Today, if it wasn't a video store or a donut shop, it was probably closed, the inside of the windows covered with brown paper, the battered doors plastered with posters which advertised some wrestling match coming to the local arena, as soon as the ice came out.

The shop where Grandpa had sold fruit and vegetables now sold yogurt and something called tofu.

"What's that?" asked Jason, making a face.

"Search me," I said.

A man in a white uniform was changing the letters on an advertisement board in the window. Behind him, we could see baskets of trailing plants hanging from the ceiling. The walls were painted pastel shades of pink and green. The place gleamed with stainless steel and glass.

But the store next to Grandpa's had the same pieces of dusty leather luggage in the window that had been there as long as I could

22

remember. The shop on the other side still sold long lengths of blood red sausage.

We drove Jason home when we took back the truck we'd rented to move our stuff. On the way, Mom took us by the school I'd be going to. I wished she hadn't.

The building was ancient, with classrooms on two floors and a schoolyard made of pavement.

"It looks like one of those correctional institutions," observed Jason, adjusting his glasses up onto his nose.

"How would you know? You ever seen one?"

"Well, no. But it looks the way I figure one'd look. You know."

"It looks the same as it did when I went to school there," said Mom. She's nearly 40, so you know how old the school had to be. "I'll bet it's still got those old wooden floors that creak."

It had and they did.

The first day, as I climbed up and down the stairs from one Grade Eight classroom to another, I started to appreciate the modern school I'd left behind—all on one floor, with skylights in the halls and grass beyond the cement in the schoolyard.

At first, the kids in the class pretty much ignored me, which was okay by me. I couldn't see any of them being my friends anyhow.

23

The homeroom teacher, a Mr. Hoskins, who had the thickest pair of glasses I'd ever seen, picked this kid named Nicholas to take me to the office to register. Probably because we were both wearing the identical sweatshirt.

"You like *Giant Squid*, too?" I asked, referring to the rock group pictured on Nicholas' chest.

"Naw. This shirt belongs to my brother," said Nicholas. "He's pretty uncool."

His only other bit of conversation, as we went down to the main floor office, was to advise me to stay out of Randy Smits' way. I'd already spotted the class troublemaker, a big kid with muscles and blonde hair that fell on one side into his eye. He sat in the back of the class with his feet stuck out into the aisle, talking in a soft voice all the while the teacher was. By the way Mr. Hoskins ignored him, just glaring at anyone who reacted to Randy's comments, it was obvious he'd given up on trying to get his co-operation.

While Nicholas went back up to class, I stayed to pick up papers for Mom to fill out and was assigned a locker. By the time I beat it back up the stairs to the next class, I was one of the last ones to enter the room.

I stood for a moment waiting for Randy and another kid who were ahead of me to go in. But Randy wasn't in any hurry. He stood in the doorway with his arm draped across the shoulder of his friend, blocking my way.

"If you don't mind..." I began, seeing the others inside, already at their desks. Showing up late in front of a roomful of strangers is not my idea of a good time.

"I do mind," said Randy. "So you just wait your turn."

"Yeah. You just wait your turn, dude," the other kid echoed.

"Are you boys coming to this class or not?" the teacher asked. And while the other two sauntered to their seats at the back of the room, I had to stand and go once more through the rigmarole of who I was and what school I'd come from.

Ms. Rabinski was the environmental studies teacher. She was very tiny and very blonde.

"Oh, Vincent Massey School," Ms. Rabinski said, raising her delicate eyebrows. "The French programme there is excellent, I hear. You'll be able to show these Grade Eights a thing or two."

I heard Randy snort and felt my face getting hot. "Not really," I mumbled. "It wasn't my best subject."

"Oh? And what was?" Was she going to make me stand there all day? Couldn't she just tell me where she wanted me to sit?

"Recess, right?" Nicholas offered, and everyone laughed. At least it broke the tension. Someone took a bunch of papers off a desk and found me a chair to go with it.

It was just my luck, when noon hour came and I went to drop off my books and pick up my lunch, that I discovered my locker was right next to Randy's. He and his friend were lounging against the opposite wall. Not waiting for me, I hoped. There are times when I wish I were invisible, and this was one of those times.

"Smart kid, eh? Where'd you come from, smart kid?" Randy came across the hall to where I was hastily shoving books onto the metal shelf over my head.

"Riverview," I said. "And I'm no 'A' student."

"Riverview. Where's that?"

"About five miles. Other side of the city."

"So why'd you come here? Old man take off?"

"We came here to live with my grandfather. He's sick and needs us."

"Anyone who'd need you would have to be sick. So where is your old man?"

"He doesn't live with us. I live with my mother." Not that it's any of your business, I wanted to say.

"That's not the question, dude. I said, where's your old man."

"Same place as yours, Randy," crowed his pal. "He goes to see him twice a month on visiting day!" And he gave Randy a punch on the shoulder that he wasn't expecting which sent him flying into me. Both of us slammed against the open door of my locker with a crash.

"Hey! Watch it, Joey!" Randy grabbed up his lunch bag off the floor and took off down the hall after his friend.

There was no place else to go and eat except the lunchroom. By the time I got there everyone was already inside. It was packed. I'd rather skip lunch than ask anyone to make room for me. I was just pushing against the door to leave again, as quietly as possible, when someone called, "Hey, Mark. Over here."

Nicholas was at one of the tables. He swept the plastic wrap piled with sandwiches along the table with his arm and moved down the bench, so I could get my legs in. Saved again. Nicholas might never become my favorite person, but anyone who rescues me from an awkward moment is a friend of mine.

"So," he said, breathing tuna fish, "How d'you like old St. Laurent Junior High?"

"Okay, I guess. School's school."

"You're right there," he said. "It sucks in any language. Randy giving you a hard time?"

"Naw. He tried to. I'm used to guys like him."

"I bet," said Nicholas, giving me a knowing elbow. "Big guy like you, eh?"

27

I hadn't yet had what Mom referred to as my growth spurt yet. That would happen in high school, she predicted. But then, neither had Nicholas.

"Just don't get in Randy's way," advised a girl with pink, spiked hair, who sat on the other side of the table.

My mother had written my name on the brown paper bag that held my lunch. "Mark Rogers," read a kid on the other side of me. "That your name?"

The girl across the table got up to leave. "Unless he's eating someone else's lunch," she said.

"This is Dennis," said Nicholas, introducing us. "The one with the mouth is Rhonda. You want to shoot a few baskets? If we hurry, we can still get one of the balls."

* * *

By the end of the first week, I knew plenty of kids. Nicholas was Nick to everyone and Rhonda was much better than her hair. Maybe it wasn't going to be too bad. It turned out that Mom had gone to school with Mr. Hoskins. She met him when she took the papers back to the office at St. Laurent .

At home, things with Grandpa were about the same, although he seemed to have stopped his wandering away. The doctor had suggested that a short walk every day with Mrs. Fuller or one of us might prevent the wandering. The daily walk seemed to be working.

He didn't sleep well at night though, and Mom and I often heard him up after we had gone to bed.

After my grandmother had died three years before, Grandpa had started sleeping in their little dining room on what Mom called a day bed, a kind of narrow couch with no arms. At the time of our move, Mom had decided to make Grandpa's choice of the dining room into a proper room for him, so Mom and I had taken the two small bedrooms upstairs with the sloping ceilings.

We'd worked all one Saturday morning to loosen the bolts that held the heavy legs on the dining room table, before moving it out to the shed. Getting Grandpa's dresser down the narrow stairs had been another tricky job. We'd hoped we'd be able to make the change with a minimum of fuss and, in fact, Grandpa hadn't even noticed.

We pushed the old day bed out into the sun room to make room for Grandpa's regular bed. The old-fashioned sideboard from the dining room suite, covered with the framed pictures of all my grandfather's family, we left alone.

He hadn't noticed what Mom and I were up to because, as usual, he was looking for something. Grandpa had this habit of setting things down and then forgetting where he put them. When he couldn't find them, he'd accuse people of stealing his stuff. Especially poor Mrs. Fuller who was with him all day. For days once he said she'd stolen his favorite belt, taken it home for one of her nephews. Who would want a worn out old belt anyway, I wondered. By the time the belt showed up, hanging behind his door, he'd forgotten he'd ever thought it was lost.

* * *

One of the things that bugged me most about living away over here at Grandpa's was that I never had any money. When we'd moved here, I'd had to give up my job at the corner variety store back on our old street. I used to go there some afternoons after school and sort pop bottles, sweep the parking lot, stuff like that. It wasn't a fancy job, but it gave me some money of my own. Things were always too tight for Mom to hand out money to me every time I needed it.

And Dad wasn't always on time with the support cheque.

I'd only been at the new school a short while when everyone started talking about our annual end-of-the-year trip. This year, because it was our graduating year, the class was planning to go to Ottawa.

I wasn't one hundred percent sure I wanted to go. But I also didn't want to be the only one who didn't go.

"All these school trips are fine," Mom agreed, "but surely not all the kids in the class can afford them."

"They've had longer to save up than I have," I pointed out. "They've known about it all year. Besides, they've already had a bake sale and a car wash to raise money." But even after that, we each had to come up with 25 dollars. I just didn't know where I was going to get that kind of money.

"You could try to get on at Hamburger Heaven," Nick suggested. "They like you to be 15, though. You'd never pass for it." Nick could afford to make useless suggestions. He already had his trip money. He baby-sat his little sister every day after school.

I decided to try around the neighbourhood to see if anyone would like me to do odd jobs for them—washing windows, cleaning garages, raking yards, whatever. I'm stronger than I look.

The man next door was sweeping the sidewalk in front of his house when I got home from school the next day. Might as well start right here, I thought.

"Hi. My name's Mark. My mom and I are living next door with my grandfather." The man didn't look up. "I need to earn some extra cash for a school trip and I was wondering if you had any odd jobs for me."

The man kept sweeping. "I could do that walk for you right now, if you like," I offered.

He gripped the broom handle tightly to him, as though he thought I was going to try to get it away from him. "Do I look like a millionaire, eh? I don't hire no kid to do my work for me."

With an attitude like that, I didn't even bother to tell him I'd work cheap.

At the next two places, there was no one home and at the last house on the block, the woman just shook her head and shrugged. I guess she couldn't understand me.

Mrs. Savalas across the street leaned her dimpled elbows on the railing of her porch and smiled. She was always nice to me. At my grandmother's funeral, she'd smothered my face with kisses and put a whole chocolate cake into the back seat of my father's car for me.

I went over to see if I could work for her. "You come and wash windows for me, Markie," she invited. "I don't pay you no cash money, but I make some nice souvlaki."

I couldn't pay my way to Ottawa with Greek cooking. I decided to try the next block tomorrow.

"Maybe if you made up a little sign, listing the jobs you could do," Mom suggested at suppertime, when I told her how my luck had been running. "People put ads up in the laundromat and supermarket all the time."

Grandpa looked up from his plate. "Who needs money? You, Giovanna?"

"Oh, you know kids, Dad," said Mom, reaching over and tucking a paper napkin into the neck of his sweater. "They always need money for something or other."

"It's no big deal, Grandpa."

My grandfather pulled the napkin out again and dribbled spaghetti sauce down his front.

"Mark will find himself a job, Dad. He's already asking on the street if there's anything."

"No work in this neighbourhood," said Grandpa. "People are poor here. But I got money, Mark."

"You, Dad? Of course, you've got your pension."

"I got money saved. You come and see me." He was finished eating and shuffled off to his room. "You come. I show you," he said.

"I can't take his money, Mom," I said.

"I know, Mark. Don't worry about it. You know he'd help you if he could. Besides, he'll probably forget he even offered it to you."

The phone rang. It was Jason. I took a handful of cookies from the table before Mom could sweep the plate away.

"I heard they were hiring at Sully's Shakes," Jason said. Back in the old neighbourhood, he was looking for an after-school job too. My old class was going to the Water Theme Park.

"We're not old enough."

"Well, Trav got on."

"He looks older. Anyhow, how would I get there?"

"Oh, yeah. I guess you couldn't."

I told him about my grandfather saying he had some money put away somewhere.

"Jeez, Mark. I heard about this old guy once who had hidden all this money in his mattress. Maybe your grandfather's rich and you guys don't even know it!"

The light was still on in Grandpa's room when I hung up the phone. The door was open, but I knocked anyway. I didn't want him to think I'd snuck up on him. Sometimes, if you startled him, he acted really weird. He might even demand to know what I was doing in his room.

"It's you, Frankie," he said when he saw me. He'd been sitting in his chair, staring at the wall in front of him.

"It's Mark, Grandpa," I said. I sure couldn't take his money with him thinking I was someone else. "Look, Grandpa." The blanket Mom had put over his knees had slipped to the floor and I picked it up. "About the money..."

Without speaking, he got up slowly and went to the tall dresser on the wall opposite the door. Opening a drawer, he pulled out a pouch made out of some soft material, yellow, like deer skin. He poked his fingers down into the bag, loosening the drawstring. Then he dumped its contents onto the bed.

Three coins. Maybe they were really old and worth a bundle, I thought.

Grandpa stepped back so that I could get a closer look, and I picked them up. Three Canadian silver dollars. Minted in the 1970's. That was all.

I stared at the coins in my palm. My grandfather was just as poor as the rest of us. Except he didn't know it.

"Thanks, Grandpa," I croaked, "but I couldn't take your money. Really."

"Why not? I want for you to have it."

"You worked hard for it. I'll just have to try harder to earn some of my own." And then I put out my arms to hug him, remembering all the times he used to hug me. Great big bear hugs they'd been, from such a small man.

Grandpa didn't hug us anymore. It upset him now when Mom or I got too close.

He folded my hand around the three coins and went back to sit in his chair. "They're yours," he said.

CHAPTER 3

The words printed on the square of pink cardboard in the window seemed to jump out at me.

"Help wanted. Person to deliver advertising flyers. Wednesdays only."

This was where the neighbourhood newspaper was printed. I propped my bike against the wall of the building and went inside. Maybe today would be my lucky day.

A long counter reached from one end of the room to the other. A man in his shirt sleeves sat in front of a computer screen, his back to me. I put my question to a thin, dark-haired girl who got up from her desk to wait on me.

"You looking for someone to deliver flyers again, Bernie?" she asked over her shoulder.

"I sure am. That last guy quit." Bernie got up and came to the counter. "Oh," he hesitated when he saw me. "Not you, I hope. We're not looking for a school kid."

"Why not? I'm a hard worker."

"These are advertisements we're talking about here. People want to see what the buys are before the stores close."

"I could be here by three-thirty every Wednesday at the latest. Why don't you give me a chance? I'm very reliable."

Bernie sighed heavily.

"If you want references," I went on, still thinking I could convince him that I could do the job, "I can give you the name of the place I worked before. I'd still be there, except we moved."

Bernie slid his hands under his suspenders and looked me over. I pulled myself up to my full height.

Someone entered the office behind me. By this time, the girl was on the telephone, so Bernie was going to have to give me an answer quickly or risk losing this other customer.

"Okay, kid," he said. "I'll give you a chance. You be here at three-thirty next Wednesday. No later. You got a bike?"

"Sure thing."

"Okay. You'll have quite a load. Have to make two or three trips. That's why I thought someone with a car would be best. But okay, you try it."

I could feel the grin spreading over my

whole face. I wanted to jump in the air and tap dance down the length of the counter. I knew Bernie wouldn't be sorry. I'd be the best darn advertising deliverer he'd ever seen.

"Can I help you?" Bernie directed his question over my head, to the person standing behind me.

I turned for the door and nearly walked right into Randy Smits.

"About the job you've got in your window," Randy said to Bernie, ignoring me. Maybe now I was invisible.

"That sign's been in the window on and off all winter and now, all of a sudden, I get two guys in here at once? I don't believe it."

"Well, is it still available?"

"You in school?"

"Yeah. Does it matter?"

"You got a car?"

"Nope. I thought I could do it on my bike."

"Well, so did he," said Bernie, jerking his thumb towards me. I waited with my hand on the door, afraid of how this might turn out. "And seeing's how I decided to give a school kid a try and he was here first, I guess the job's his."

I opened the door quickly, before Bernie could change his mind. "It'll be mine the minute this weenie messes up," growled Randy, elbowing past and not even holding the door for me.

* * *

"The man doesn't pay enough to attract someone with a car," Mom grumbled when I told her that evening about my new job. "Who does he think he is, exploiting children."

"It's not like that, Mom. He didn't want a kid, but I persuaded him to let me try."

She was not impressed, having decided already that it was going to create a problem with Grandpa.

"It's only one afternoon a week." Why did she have to run it down? I knew I could do it. I wished she had more faith in me.

"Well, it's up to you, Mark, to ask Mrs. Fuller to stay late on Wednesdays. That's the only way you can possibly do it. You know we count on you to be here by four o'clock to take over."

No problem. Wasn't Mom always saying that I had Mrs. Fuller wrapped around my little finger? She thought I was just the cutest thing. She made me chocolate chip cookies and stuff like that all the time. She'd even pinch my cheeks if I'd let her.

As soon as Mrs. Fuller had hung her jacket up the next morning and gone to the kitchen to start Grandpa's breakfast, I asked her about staying late on Wednesdays. "Just until I get some flyers delivered in the neighbourhood," I explained. "I've got myself a job now, to help out and stuff. It'll only be one afternoon a week."

"The six o'clock bus is the latest one I can catch and not miss my connections," she said, stirring an egg with a fork in a tea cup.

"I'm sure to have them all delivered by six. If not, I can do the rest after Mom gets home."

"Well, I guess it'll be all right. I'm really glad you got the job, Mark." She patted my head as if I were a puppy. This once, I didn't care; she was the key to me holding this job.

"But not this Wednesday," she remembered. "I've got an appointment at four-thirty, so I have to catch my regular bus. We'll start the new arrangement the week after. Okay?"

I hadn't figured on this. Bernie wanted me to start this week. My mind went into high gear. There must be some way I could do it. "Okay," I agreed. "Thanks, Mrs. F." I was sure if I thought hard enough I'd come up with something.

"Glad I can help," she chirped.

Grandpa should be all right for one afternoon, I thought. I'd deliver the flyers closest to home first, so I could check on him. If he was okay, and I was sure he would be, I'd go back for another load. He'd been pretty good lately. It didn't make sense that he'd pick this one afternoon to mess up.

41

"Everything okay with Mrs. Fuller?" Mom asked when she got in from work.

"All looked after," I said, stretching the truth just a little.

"I didn't mean to put such a damper on your job, honey," said Mom, giving me a kiss on the forehead. "I'm really proud of you." She should have kicked me instead; it would have made me feel better. "You've helped all of us adjust to this new living arrangement like an adult. And thanks for setting the table," she added, with a note of surprise in her voice. I had felt that it was the least I could do.

* * *

On Wednesday, I picked up my first load of advertising flyers a few minutes before three-thirty and peddled away up the street to the top of our block.

It was an easy job—just stick a flyer into every mailbox or slot. It was a nice, bright May afternoon. A lot of people were outside, so that I was able to put their flyers right into their hands. I could tell by the look on their faces that they were not used to such personal service.

"Have a nice day," I said for the twenty-fifth time. Nobody had told me to say that. It had worked at the supermarket and it seemed like the right thing to do.

"Hey, how'd you get the job, Mark?" Nick was coming up the street with his little sister, Jessie.

"I applied for it," I yelled.

"Hiya, Mark." Jessie waved a small hand as I passed.

"Lucky stiff," said Nick.

"Sure beats baby-sitting," I razzed him.

At four-fifteen exactly, I dropped my bike on the back steps of our place and went inside. "I'm here," I called, not too loudly.

"Good boy," said Mrs. Fuller. She already had her jacket on, the plastic shopping bag with her knitting in it over her arm. "I'm on my way, then. Your Grandpa is having a nice nap this afternoon."

I went through to close the front door behind her and watched while she trotted off up the street to the bus stop. I could see Grandpa curled up like a baby on his bed, the afghan moving slowly up and down with his breathing. I knew Mom liked to keep his daytime nap short so that he'd sleep better at night. But I wasn't going to be the one to rouse him now.

I closed the back door gently and took my bike with its load of flyers out through the back way to the next street.

That load delivered in record time, I went back up our street to check on Grandpa. I rode up the walk and let my bike down onto the steps. Then I walked softly through to his room.

He wasn't there.

"Grandpa?" I called. "Hey, Grandpa. It's me. Mark."

I stuck my head into the empty bathroom and walked on out to the kitchen. "Must be out back," I figured. He used to love to putter around in his tool shed, before Mom started locking it, in case he got out there and hurt himself.

The padlock was still on the shed and the yard was deserted. Now, I started to worry. As I turned to go back inside, I saw that the side gate was open. I knew I'd shut it when I'd come back the first time.

Cripes, it wasn't even five o'clock yet. Where could he have gone in such a short time? Sweat prickled in my armpits and the palms of my hands. This couldn't be happening. If Grandpa had gotten hurt, it would be all my fault.

My heart hammering so loud I could hear it, I banged on the door of the house next door.

"What is it?" I heard Mr. Singh come scuffing down the hall towards the door in his slippers, saw him rubbing his eyes. I'd woken him up.

He wouldn't have seen my grandfather if he'd been sleeping.

"What do you want?" he demanded, opening the door.

I was already back out to the sidewalk. "Forget it," I yelled, overcome by fear. "I'm looking for someone." I hesitated, looking both ways up the street. A group of little kids was playing with a skipping rope at the corner. "You see Luigi Cecchini come by?" I asked.

"Nope," they said and kept turning the rope, beating the dust.

Mrs. Savalas across the street was shaking a rug out over the side of her porch. "You see my grandfather?" I called.

She shook her head. "Not today, Markie."

I'd have to take my bike and go up and down the streets, looking for him.

"Are you looking for Luigi?" our neighbour on the other side asked when I ran back and picked up the bike. "I saw him go up the other way."

"Why didn't you stop him?"

"I thought he was following that lady who comes to his place every day."

Mrs. Fuller. He must have followed her to the bus stop the minute I went out the back way, thought it was time for his walk. Well, at least I knew the direction he'd gone.

I rode as hard as I could to the stop lights at the four corners. Which way would he go? He couldn't have boarded the bus with Mrs. Fuller or she'd have brought him back.

Why did this have to happen today, of all days? My first day on the job. And just when everything seemed to be going so well.

I had started south again on the next street when suddenly I spotted him. He wasn't moving very fast; he never did anymore. Even from two blocks away I knew it was him.

Relief flooded through me, turning my legs to rubber. I rode up beside him and stopped. "Grandpa?"

He looked up at me and I realized at once that he didn't recognize me. "It's me. Mark. Come on, Grandpa. I'll take you home."

Obediently, he took my arm, but the way he kept looking at me and smiling shyly, I could have been anybody. I was really scared now. What had I done? I'd never seen him look this bad.

And then I saw that all he had on his feet were his socks. That Mrs. Fuller. This was all her fault. She had been the one who had suggested taking his shoes away so that he'd stay home.

I forgot about the flyers waiting to be delivered. I just had to get my grandfather home before Mom found out, but it was impossible to hurry him. He moved like a robot, one stockinged foot in front of the other.

We passed a group of kids from school hanging out at the store on the corner. "Hey, Rogers," someone shouted. "Did the old guy escape again?"

Grandpa turned his same pathetic smile on them as we passed, me holding my bike up and him shuffling along beside me, his hand through my arm. The only thing I could be thankful for was that he was not resisting me.

We met Mom coming up the street. It couldn't have been worse timing. "Mark! Dad! What on earth?"

"He's okay, Mom."

"Dad? Come on in, dear. Come inside."

There wasn't much left to the soles of Grandpa's socks. I stood in the corner of his room while Mom peeled them off and lifted his feet into a basin of warm water. She sat back on her heels and looked at me. "How did this happen, Mark?"

"I guess it was my fault, Mom. I left him alone to deliver the flyers. But only for a few minutes."

"You what? Where was Mrs. Fuller? I thought you said you'd worked things out between you."

"I didn't think it would hurt, Mom. Honest. She had to leave at her regular time tonight. He was only alone for a few minutes. I was here when Mrs. Fuller left, and then I went as fast as I could."

Mom interrupted me with a voice like ice. "Get me a towel for your grandfather's feet, Mark. We'll talk about this after supper."

Actually, we didn't talk. She didn't speak to me for hours. And I didn't have anything to say either.

From upstairs in my room, I heard her come into the hall and dial the telephone. I crept to the top of the stairs to listen. Who was she going to tell about me being a liar?

"I see," I heard Mom say. "Yes, I see." Then she gave a sigh. "No, it certainly isn't your fault, Mrs. Fuller. He put this job of his before his family responsibilities." Not one word about Grandpa being outside in his socks, thanks to her brilliant idea. Mom hung up the receiver and went into the kitchen.

I felt terrible. Of course, Mom was right. She hadn't liked the idea of this job all along. In my own defense, I had good reason for what I had done, but I knew my motives didn't really count for anything.

I stayed in my room until I could stand it no longer. I had to do something about the flyers that were still waiting to be delivered. When I came downstairs Mom had cleaned up the meal and was loading clothes into the washer.

48

"You can cook yourself some eggs," she said. "Your grandfather and I have already eaten."

"Is he okay, Mom?"

"He's all right. No thanks to you."

"Mom, I'm really sorry."

"I guess I was wrong, Mark. I said you were acting like an adult. Responsible. I'd forgotten you're still a child."

I sat down and started picking at the threads on the place where the thighs of my jeans were wearing thin. How could I put this? "I still have to deliver the rest of the flyers, Mom. Please understand."

She hesitated a moment and then poured the detergent into the machine.

"I'm sorry I let you down. I let everyone down. But I have to keep this job. You know I do. It'll only take me a half hour to finish up tonight."

"I'm sorry too, Mark." She leaned against the washer with her arms folded. "Sorry that you think money is more important than the people who are counting on you."

"It isn't like that," I argued. "But the man at the newspaper office is counting on me, too. You don't want me to let him down, do you?"

"You do what you like," she said coldly and left the room.

Maybe Mom was letting me make my own decision. Of *course* money wasn't as important as Grandpa. But it was something we couldn't do without. I sat for a minute hearing the thump-swish, thump-swish of the washing machine. What else could I do? Hadn't Mom always told me to finish whatever job I started?

It was almost nine when I put my bike away and came back inside the house. Mom had gone to bed. I was glad of that. I just wanted to put the whole episode behind me. Start all over again. But I knew no one was going to let me forget it this easily.

CHAPTER 4

In the lunchroom the next day a bunch of us Grade Eights were eating together when Randy, who was at the next table, looked up at me and asked, in a loud voice, "Crazy Luigi your grandfather, Rogers?"

I hadn't seen Randy among the group at the corner store last night, but I guessed someone had told him what had happened.

"That old guy's off his rocker," Randy announced. "He should be in a rubber room. You know what everyone around here calls him, don't you? Crazy Luigi. Hey, Joey," he yelled, although Joey was sitting right next to him, "Roger's grandfather is Crazy Luigi!"

My eyes met Joey's and he looked quickly away. No one had to tell me who had told Randy about seeing us last night. "Leave him alone, Randy, okay?" Joey muttered.

"Hey, what's with you?"

"Just lay off." Joey got up from the table, balled up his lunch bag and fired it at the garbage can. Then he went out through the swinging doors.

"Hey, where are you going?" Randy started after his friend. "Oh, forget it," he decided. He turned to anyone else who'd listen. "Hey, Rhonda. You know old Crazy Luigi?"

"You're a creep, Randy," said Rhonda.

"What'd I do? You guys all saw him. Didn't they tell you about the time Roger's grandfather went walking down the street, naked as a jay bird?"

I could feel everyone looking at me now, my face getting red. No one at our table said anything, but I could hear kids snickering in other parts of the room. I wanted to crawl into a hole and die.

Before I knew what was happening, Nick put a hand under my elbow and propelled me out of the lunchroom. "I should have punched his face in," I said when we were alone.

"He's just ignorant," Nick said.

"Is it true what he said?"

"Yeah," said Nick. "I guess."

"He really was naked?" This was the very worst thing I could have imagined.

Nick shrugged. "I guess so."

"And the whole school knows?"

"It was a long time ago. Before you moved here."

This was too much. Maybe Randy was right. Maybe my grandfather was ready for the nut house. "I'm going back inside," I said, feeling sick.

"I'll go with you."

"No. Thanks anyway. I'm not going to hit anyone." I just didn't want any company right then. I wanted to run as far away from here as I could get. Instead, I walked right on out the front door of the school and went home.

I lay on my bed all afternoon. Mrs. Fuller came and tapped softly on my door. "Are you all right, Mark?"

I told her I wasn't feeling good and she left me alone then. I heard Nick when he brought my bike home for me, but I didn't even go to the top of the stairs to hear what he told Mrs. Fuller.

The kids called my grandfather Crazy Luigi. I know that didn't hurt him, but it sure hurt me. How could they? He wasn't crazy; he was just a sick old man. Never hurt anyone in his life. He'd worked hard all those years, probably fed half the people in this neighbourhood. And this was how their kids treated him.

But wasn't I feeling the same way the others were? No matter how sorry I felt for him, I couldn't get out of my mind the fact that my grandfather was ruining my life. And I couldn't erase the picture of his skinny, wrinkled old body, wandering around the streets, stark naked.

I went and sat with him when Mrs. Fuller left and watched while he took twenty minutes to peel an orange with a dull knife and slowly eat the segments off the side of the blade. How could anyone change as much as he had?

* * *

On Wednesday, I went again to the newspaper office. "My flyers?" I asked the girl at the desk. The week before they had been stacked inside the door.

"Hold on a minute." Bernie came around the counter. "You have some kind of a problem last week?"

"A problem?"

"Yeah. A problem. I had people phoning me about not getting their flyers until after dark. No little old lady wants a kid poking around her mail slot in the middle of the night. You let me down. I should have known a kid couldn't do this job."

"I had an emergency, sir. With my grandfather."

"Your grandfather," he repeated, nodding as if it could only be a lie. "I see. An emergency."

"Yes, sir. He's sick and I was supposed to

54

look after him. I did deliver the flyers, sir. Every last one of them. I know it was late. I swear it won't happen again. Please give me another chance."

He just stood there, shaking his head. Unable to believe my nerve was my guess. "Well, kid. No one can say I'm not a fair man. I will give you another chance. But it's your last."

"Thank you, sir. I won't disappoint you."

"Go on, then. Your flyers are out back at the loading door."

"You sure you can manage all those?" the man out back asked, as he watched me fill my canvas bag with papers.

"I sure can. And I'll be back for the rest in an hour." And off I went.

Gratefully, I filled my lungs with the fresh, spring air. From now on, I told myself, peddling hard, if I had anything to do with it, things were going to start to look up. Bernie had given me another chance to prove myself, and Mom had told me that if Bernie hadn't already fired me, I could keep my job. Providing I held my end up at home.

We were trying to treat Grandpa with dignity, and that was all that mattered. It wasn't such a rotten life, after all.

The heavy bag made balancing difficult. It was a relief to get the first half delivered. I had hoped to be able to get rid of them all in a couple of hours, but at a quarter to six I still had about 25 papers to go. I'd have to try to shave that time down. If I hadn't wasted time persuading Bernie to keep me on, I'd have made it. With practice, I was sure to get faster. Besides, there must be some shortcuts through the neighbourhood I didn't know about yet. I'd have to ask Nick.

I went home so that Mrs. Fuller could get her bus. I was dishing out the casserole when Mom got in a few minutes later. "How'd the job go today?" she asked, letting her purse down inside the kitchen door.

"Great," I said. "Bernie's giving me another chance. I've just got one street left."

"Then you go and look after it. I know time is important in this job."

"Thanks, Mom. Okay if I eat later?"

"Sure. I'll get your grandfather fed. You go and look after the rest of the ads. Here, better take a piece of bread with you. Keep your strength up."

We were friends again. She slapped some margarine on the bread for me and I went out through the back, folding the food into my mouth.

I went through to the next street and rode straight south. Two blocks down, I could cut through the laneway and get onto the last street.

I was just coming around a row of dumpsters when I nearly ran into Randy Smits. He was standing at the end of the lane, his bike between his legs, both feet firmly on the ground.

"Forget it, pal," he said, as I made to go past him. "This is my street."

"Since when?"

"Anything you want delivered on this street, I'll deliver."

"Come off it, Randy. You're just sore because I got the job. Now let me through." With things going as well as they had today, I found courage I didn't know I had.

"You've gone as far as you're going, Rogers." He let his own bike drop and reached over to grab my handlebars. "You take your papers and get lost."

He wasn't fooling around. I was no match for him and, courageous or not, I knew it. "Okay, okay. Just let me go."

I turned and headed back up the lane. If I could just cut through someone's yard, I could get out to the street. But I wasn't familiar with these houses yet. Instead, I rode to the next block and started down the sidewalk. I'd delivered this part of the street already.

I had reached the first house in the final block when Randy came swooping out between that one and the next and deliberately collided with my bike.

"Hey! Get lost!" I yelled, tripping myself up in the bicycle.

"*You* get lost, Rogers," he said between clenched teeth. "I told you, you aren't delivering on this street."

"Look," I said, hoping my voice didn't betray me. My insides were doing back springs. "What does it matter to you? It's just a two-bit job. You can get on at the hamburger place, no sweat. Anyone'd think for sure you were 15."

"Take off, Rogers," he ordered. "And remember this, no one makes me look like a creep in front of my friends."

So that was it. Joey and the others had turned on him for picking on my grandfather last week.

"Look, you want to deliver the ads, you deliver them." And I started to lift the canvas bag off the bike. With one shove, Randy knocked me, the bag and the bike to the ground again. The chain sprocket bit into the flesh on the inside of my ankle, stinging like crazy.

I'd had enough; I'm not a fighter. Without even looking at him, I picked up my bike with trembling arms and headed back up the street. There was no way I was going to get past him. I forced myself not to look back over my shoulder, in case he was following me, and I walked away as quickly as my stinging ankle would allow.

It was dark now and I had almost 25 papers folded and ready to deliver in my bag. What was I going to do with them? As I crossed back to my own street I saw a plastic garbage can set out by someone's fence for morning. Taking the flyers out of my bag, I set them down into the can and placed the lid carefully back on top. Sure, I knew it was cheating, but the way I saw it, I had no other choice.

Back at the house, I looked at the plate of supper Mom had set in the fridge for me, but I'd lost my appetite. I went into the bathroom and examined my ankle. It hadn't bled much. It was one of those cuts that didn't have to in order to hurt. I dabbed at it with a face cloth and put a bandaid over the worst part of it. Why did Randy have to be such a total jerk?

"Six, under the basket," said Grandpa at the bathroom door, startling me.

"What did you say, Grandpa?"

"You know," he said.

"No. I didn't hear you."

"About the beetles," he said.

"About what beetles?"

"You know," he insisted, twisting his hands and looking as if he were going to cry.

"You okay, Grandpa?" But he had walked away.

More and more, what he said wasn't making sense, but if you tried to understand, tried to get him to repeat what he'd said, he just got angry or started to cry like a two-year-old.

I didn't sleep much that night. I'm not sure if it was my empty stomach keeping me awake, the encounter with Randy or the wind that seemed to be getting stronger every hour. The loose tin on the roof of the shed out back flapped furiously. I heard Mom go downstairs to check on Grandpa more than once.

She'd had new locks installed on the front and back doors, had removed everything we could think of as potentially dangerous to him, even put childproof latches on the kitchen cabinets. But still she worried about him.

* * *

In the morning, after Mom left for work and before Mrs. Fuller arrived, Grandpa came out of his room with his pants on over his pyjamas.

"Come on, Grandpa," I said. "I'll help you get dressed."

He looked down at himself, surprised.

"Why don't you wear the track pants Mom

got for you?"

Deliberately ignoring me, he sat down at the kitchen table to wait for Mrs. Fuller. Every weekday morning, she made his breakfast and helped him to eat it. Then she'd lead him to the sink with the mirror over it in the corner of the kitchen. One by one, she would hand him the things he needed to shave with—the cup with the soap in it, the wet brush, the safety razor. It was this daily routine, now much slower than ever, that kept Grandpa on track. With his mind the way it was, he was only capable of doing one task at a time and couldn't remember the last thing he had done.

I looked at him sitting there at the table, his back still as straight as a rod, his pyjamas sticking out over his socks.

It was Nick coming to the door that distracted me from my thoughts. Mrs. Fuller was right behind him. Now she could decide whether the way Grandpa was dressed was important enough to worry about.

"What's happening, man?" Nick asked in a low, urgent voice. "Your papers are all over the place."

"My papers?" I stepped outside.

The wind last night had brought down a lot of smaller tree branches onto front porches and lawns and had hurled garbage cans down the street. Papers were everywhere.

"Those flyers are yours and they're all over everyone's yards," Nick said.

"Oh, no!" I pulled the door shut behind us. "I put the ones I couldn't deliver into a garbage can. The wind must have blown it over in the night. What a mess!" I could hardly pretend the papers weren't mine. That bright ink and bold lettering couldn't be anything else.

"Well, come on. I'll help you. We can catch a few before they get away on us."

Nick and I raced against the wind, fishing papers out from puddles under parked cars, off fences and hedges and unwrapping them from hydro poles. We picked up as many as we could, but there always seemed to be more in the next yard.

It was getting late. I took Nick's armload of tattered paper from him. "Go on ahead. I'll get my books and catch up."

After the episode with Randy the night before, the front wheel of my bike was bent out of shape and it wobbled all the way to school. Before I got there, the chain came off. Now I was going to have to have money to get my bicycle fixed.

* * *

"Why is all that paper out in the shed?" Mom asked, when she had been out there to fetch the mop for the floor.

"They were blowing down the street this morning and Nick and I picked them up. We were late for school, so I just threw them into the shed." I got up from the table. "I meant to put them into the garbage after school. I'll go and do it now."

Mom followed me outside. There was no escaping her. "They're your papers, aren't they, Mark? What's this all about? Why were they blowing all over the neighbourhood this morning?"

When I told her what had happened, she just shook her head. "You're going to have to get through to that boy somehow or other. You can't allow him to stop you from doing your job."

"Right, Mom. I'll just tell him to leave me alone."

"You want me to call him?"

"No, of course not!"

"By rights, he should pay to have your bike fixed. Just look at it. You're going to need it next Wednesday."

"Well, no one's going to get him to pay for it. That's for sure. You don't understand how it is, Mom. He's this great big guy, a real gorilla."

"All I know is that this gorilla is keeping you from doing the job you agreed to do."

* * *

On Saturday, Nick and I were just goofing around together when we decided to go to the store on the corner. "Let's go in and see if they've got any new skateboarding magazines," Nick suggested. We were both interested in the sport, though neither one of us owned a board. The week before, we'd been over to the parking lot at the supermarket to watch the kids who were really good at it. A skateboard was another thing a kid needed money for.

"Hey!" A heavy woman carrying a plastic jug of milk put a hand on my arm inside the store, stopping me cold. "Aren't you the kid who's supposed to be bringing me the advertising papers?"

I had no idea who this person was. "I-I suppose," I stammered.

"So where are they?"

"Where's what?" I could see that Nick had reached the magazine rack at the back of the store and was already starting to browse. You had to be fast, before the clerk told you to buy or get lost.

"My papers."

"Oh. What street are you on?"

"437 Jamieson."

"I'm sorry, Ma'am. I guess I didn't deliver on that part of the street last week."

"No, I guess you didn't. And you missed the Chang's down the block and Estelle on the other side."

"Sorry."

"You aren't going to keep that job long if that's the way you look after it." She heaved herself out through the narrow aisle to the door.

"Whew!" I exclaimed, joining Nick in front of the magazines. "Was she steamed!"

"Oh, man. That's really weird," he grinned. "You know who that was?"

"Nope. Who?"

"Mrs. Smits. Randy's mother."

"You're kidding. I should have told her why I didn't deliver her flyer, then."

"You wouldn't dare."

"No. But I'd like to." And all the way home, Nick and I thought up ways to get even with Randy Smits, each one more humiliating than the last. Revenge, even if it's only in the mind, is sweet.

That night when Mom called up to my room to tell me there was a man on the phone, I knew it could only be Bernie. I came down the stairs, inch by inch.

"If you come in on Monday," Bernie said in a very formal tone, "I'll give you your pay. Then you and I can have a talk."

I knew I'd lost my job; I'd known it for days. If I hadn't wanted my pay, I wouldn't have gone in. Why suffer the humiliation of a "talk."

"I know what you want to say," I told Bernie, when he faced me over the counter at the newspaper office.

"Smart kid," he said and shoved a small, brown pay envelope at me over the polished surface. "Then you also know why I have to let you go."

I nodded. But I could see he was going to tell me anyway. "Too many complaints, kid. Too many people who didn't get their flyers. Must have had a dozen of 'em."

"I'd like to explain," I said.

"Okay. Shoot."

"There was this guy," I began. "He wouldn't let me deliver on his street." Now it all sounded pretty unbelievable. Childish too. "You remember the guy who wanted this job? Well, it's him. Said he'd knock my head off if I did. I know it sounds stupid."

Bernie let out a long sigh and snapped his suspenders. "Well, kid, that's too bad. I guess a grown-up wouldn't have had that type of problem. Look, you tried. But I have to let you go."

"Thanks," I said and pocketed the envelope, relieved that at last I was going to be getting out of there.

"See you, Mark," said the girl at the keyboard, without looking up.

On the way home, I tore the top off the envelope. Inside was 16 dollars.

* * *

"There are a few people who don't have their trip money in yet," Mr. Hoskins announced to the home room next day. "It all has to be in one week from today. See me if you anticipate a problem."

There was going to be a problem all right. How was I going to come up with nine more dollars? It might as well have been 90, the way my luck was running. I waited my turn by Mr. Hoskin's desk.

CHAPTER 5

Every year, the schools around here make the kids do public speaking. I know there's probably a good reason behind the plan, but for some of us, the only thing worse than thinking up a halfway interesting topic is having to get up in front of the whole class and deliver it.

I'd hoped maybe I'd missed this special agony by moving from one school to another, but no such luck. Mr. Hoskins did put my name at the very end of the list, but he made it plain that he expected me to deliver, nonetheless. My turn was coming.

A couple of times a week now, we were treated to someone's effort in the field of public speaking. This afternoon, it was Rhonda's turn, and judging from her appearance, I expected it to be 'way out of left field'. Instead, it was really neat.

She stood up in front of the class and talked

about her little brother who had been born with Down's syndrome. She talked about how, in the old days, people used to hide anyone who was different, keep them home where no one could stare. But life for Bobby and his family was better. He was a happy, loveable kid. She had pictures of him getting on the school bus and going to his special kindergarten.

"The only people who make fun of anyone like Bobby," Rhonda concluded, "are people who don't understand. People who are afraid of what they don't know about."

When she went back to her seat, the class was absolutely quiet. Then, clearing his throat noisily, Mr. Hoskins came back to the front of the room. "You've shown courage in picking your topic, Rhonda," he said, "and you've taught us all something. Knowledge is the key."

He wrote on the board, "Enlightenment brings understanding." He continued, "This is true about many things. We are afraid of that about which we know little. Don't let ignorance be the reason for your fear."

Rhonda's speech was the topic of conversation between Nick and me as we walked home from school that afternoon. "She'll get 'A' for sure," I predicted.

"I still like the funny speeches best," Nick said.

"Mr. Hoskins doesn't."

"You could do that too, you know."

"Do what? I'm no comedian."

"I mean, make a speech like Rhonda's."

"I don't know anyone with Down's syndrome." But I've seen kids like Bobby, and now I know what it's called.

"I mean about your grandfather. And that disease he has."

"Alzheimer's. Yeah. I suppose." I had to present my speech next Friday. It would be an unusual topic, all right. And it was something I was learning more about every day. "I might," I said.

Mom thought it would be a terrific subject for my talk. "Go to the library," she urged. "Do some research. Maybe you'll find someone has written a book on the subject that the general public can understand."

"I'm not sure it's such a great idea," I hesitated. "They make fun of Grandpa, you know. They call him Crazy Luigi."

"Because they don't understand, Mark. You could be the one to change that. What was that you said about enlightenment?"

You have to watch what you say to mothers. Things have a way of coming back to haunt you.

The very next morning, before I lost my nerve, I told Mr. Hoskins what I'd chosen for my speech. "That's perfect, Mark," he said. "I'll be looking forward to it. And Mark," he remembered, as I was going to my desk, "tell us what it's like for you, living with someone who has Alzheimer's."

What was it like for me, exactly?

Over the next few days, I did read some stuff on the subject. Mom had some brochures about it at home that she'd been given by her support group, and I found a book on Alzheimer's in the library. But mostly, I just watched Grandpa.

When I had written it all out, I gave it to Mom to proofread. If she liked it, I only had to do it in point form on cue cards and then learn it. We lost marks if we read the whole thing.

Mom brought the papers back up to me in my room. "It made me cry," she admitted. I didn't know if that was a good sign or not.

* * *

The last Friday in May, when we came back into school after the noon recess, it was my turn to give my speech. It was not the best time to get everyone's attention. We were all warm and dusty and more than a little tired from a game of softball in the schoolyard. Someone opened all the windows in the classroom, and we waited for a hint of a breeze to cool us.

"Mark's grandfather has Alzheimer's disease," said Mr. Hoskins, writing the word on the board. I could see one or two kids with their heads down on their desks already.

"We're learning more about this disease all the time, but we still haven't pinpointed what causes it." Then he wrote "Mr. Luigi Cecchini" on the board and turned around to face the class. Had he heard about "Crazy Luigi," I wondered.

"Most of you know Mark's grandfather," he said, playing with the chalk. Then, "Straighten up, Richards! You too, Smits! Mr. Cecchini has been an important part of this community for many years. But don't just take my word for it. Ask your parents if Luigi Cecchini's tomatoes weren't the biggest and the sweetest, his lettuce the freshest in the city. Okay, Mark. You're on."

"The grandfather that I remember best," I began, "was a little Italian with a quick temper and an even quicker smile." (I have to give Mom credit for my opening line.) "When I was a little kid I used to come and visit him, hang around his store, take the wrappers off the tomatoes, clean up the lettuce leaves from the floor, anything so as to be near him. When I got older, my friend Jason and I would ride over here on the bus and the streetcar to see what we could do for him. Afterwards, he'd take us out for spaghetti. Then we'd all go back to his place and get bawled out by my grandmother who had kept supper waiting for us."

I had their attention now. Maybe I wasn't the only one who had an Italian grandmother.

"Grandpa gave away almost as much of his produce as he sold. Grandma used to yell at him about that, too. But she was just as generous, always baking for the neighbours or serving suppers in the church basement." People aren't like that much today. Except here in this neighbourhood.

"My grandfather isn't anything like that anymore. He looks about the same. I guess because he doesn't really look sick, people think he must be crazy to act the way he does. He certainly does some crazy things." I heard someone shift uncomfortably in the back.

"These days my grandfather doesn't smile. Sometimes he doesn't even know who we are. And when he does speak, the words come out all wrong.

"His housekeeper takes him for a walk every day. The doctor said it might stop his wandering away. But he's having trouble moving now, so he can't go far. We have to help him get dressed. He doesn't like this. If he dresses himself, we have to tell him what piece of clothing to put on next. Because he is what is called 'memory impaired', he can't remember what happened just a few minutes ago. If we weren't there, he'd forget to eat even. Part of the brain of a person with Alzheimer's has been destroyed. It will never get better.

"We've taken all the floor mats out of the house so he won't slip on them. We've had railings put on his bed, so he can't roll out, and one to hang onto in the bathtub.

"This disease can strike people as young as our parents, although most people who get it are over 65. We really aren't sure when it started with my grandfather. Maybe when my grandmother died, maybe before. He sold his store when he started getting too confused to look after it properly.

"Sometimes my grandfather gets really angry. We didn't know he knew all the swear words he uses." This brought some laughter from the kids in the class. "When he was well, my grandfather never swore. We know it's because he can't do or say the things he wants to. And he gets angriest at us, the people who do everything for him. It's hard not to get mad back at him. Sometimes I do. Then I just have to walk away. But only if there's someone else there to keep an eye on him. They say it's a 36 hour a day job, and it seems that it is.

"My mother and I know that eventually we won't be able to do all the things that need to be done for him. When he gets too sick, we'll have to find a place for him in a nursing home. People with Alzheimer's disease sometimes live as long as 15 years after diagnosis. A true diagnosis can only be made after death."

I'd found this out in one of the brochures. Only by an autopsy of the diseased brain tissue could the doctors say for sure that the person had had Alzheimer's. Grandpa had had all sorts of tests to eliminate other causes of what was called 'dementia.'

"I didn't want to move here. To have to be home every day after school to look after him. But every time I remember what good times we'd had, the way my grandfather was before he got sick, I know I don't want to have to put him in a nursing home. Not yet."

I looked up, felt the colour rise in my face, my pulse quicken. I wasn't sure I was going to say this next part, but Mom had said if I were going to give a clear picture of the disease, I should. "It's not easy living with someone with Alzheimer's," I admitted. "No one likes to think about a 70 year-old man who wets his pants."

To my intense relief, no one laughed.

I was just glad it was over. I knew I'd kept my nose too close to my cue cards, but I did come up with a good solid 'B' in the end. I was glad it was Rhonda's speech which won. Now she was going to have to give it in front of the whole school. And if she won that competition, then who knows where she'd have to go. Public speaking wasn't my best subject, either.

Mr. Hoskins liked my speech so well, that he asked me if he could use it for the school newspaper. Mom was so pleased that she took it to work with her and typed it out properly before I gave it to him.

* * *

When I got home from school about a week later, there was a blue car in front of the house. There weren't many places to park in this neighbourhood so there were always cars on the street. But this one was newer, flashier than the ones I was used to seeing. It had tinted windows and sparkling, metallic paint.

My dad was sitting in the kitchen, having coffee like one of the family. Mrs. Fuller was holding a cup to Grandpa's lips and he was slurping noisily.

Dad got up and, smiling, reached out for me. "Mark. How are you, son?"

You know that feeling you get sometimes when someone who used to be important to you suddenly shows up? And you feel as if he's intruding, going to spoil everything you've gotten used to? That's how I felt, seeing my dad in our kitchen.

"Hi," I said. "I didn't know you were coming." I held onto my book bag rather than return his hug. Now that I was older, I was beginning to view my dad's rare appearances with some suspicion.

"Didn't know myself. I had business here at the last minute."

"Richard," said Grandpa.

"See," beamed Mrs. Fuller, touching Grandpa's bib to his mustache, "he remembered your father's name. Knew him right off."

"Boy, will Mom ever be surprised." I set my bag down and lowered myself onto a chair. I wasn't sure how well she was going to take this surprise, either. As far as I knew, she and my dad hadn't seen each other in months, and their few telephone conversations were usually angry ones, over him not sending the support money on time.

"She knows already. Your Mom's upstairs, son."

"How come?"

77

"She isn't well. Didn't you know?"

"I knew she was tired. I didn't know she was sick."

"Too sick to go in to work today." My father's voice followed me as I hurried up the stairs.

Mom was lying huddled under a heap of blankets on her bed. She didn't move when I entered the room. I went to the side of the bed to look at her.

"Mark." Her eyelids fluttered open. "Hi, honey." Her eyes were sunk in dark circles of fatigue.

"Are you okay, Mom?"

"Just tired, dear. Very, very tired." Her eyelids slid slowly shut.

"How come Dad's here?" But she had fallen asleep again and didn't hear me.

"She called me, son." Dad was standing in the doorway.

"Called you? Why?"

"S'okay, honey." Mom let a hand trail off the bed, brushing my hip, reassuring me. She kept her eyes closed.

"Come on, Mark. Let's let her sleep. Come on downstairs where you and I can talk."

I hadn't seen Mom like this before. Well, maybe I had and had just gotten used to it. "What's the matter with her?" I asked, as we went back into the kitchen. I could see Mrs. Fuller outside with Grandpa. His daily excursions now had shrunk to the length of the front walk. He held Mrs. Fuller's arm with both hands and shuffled to the end of the sidewalk.

"The doctor says it's exhaustion," said Dad, pouring himself another cup of coffee. He'd brought a box of donuts with him, and he shoved it across the table to me. "Have one, son."

I shook my head.

"Come on, you look as though you could do with a few extra pounds."

"You called the doctor?" I persisted.

"No. He came by to see your grandfather on his way to the hospital. Mrs. Fuller was worried about your mother, so the doctor had a look at her. You know your mother. Never takes a day off work, never gives in."

Didn't he realize that she had to work just so the three of us could live?

"Actually, I'm worried about her too, Mark. Looking after your Grandpa Luigi has really taken a toll on her."

I looked up from the salt and pepper shakers I'd been sliding around each other on the surface of the table. Now they squared off, ready to fight. "Since when did you care anything about my mother?" I said softly.

Dad threw his head back and looked at the ceiling. "I thought you and I had put all that behind us," he said. And he was right. I guess

I was just upset at finding Mom at home, sick. "Your mother called me, Mark."

I backed off a bit then. "That's what I don't understand," I admitted.

"Oh, it was a while ago, to talk about Luigi. She wasn't sick at the time, but wanted me to let her know when I'd be down this way again. So here I am. It's time, Mark. Time we started looking for a place where your grandfather can have constant care."

"He's okay here."

"For now. But we have to think about the future."

"The three of us can manage."

"It's killing your mother, son. And it must be affecting you."

"No, not really."

"There must be things you'd like to be able to do with your friends and can't."

"Come off it, Dad!" I got up, shoving my chair into the wall behind me. "We moved here to look after him. We knew it was going to be like this."

But had we really known? It was much harder than I'd imagined it could be. I hadn't seen Jason or Travis in weeks, and I never invited Nick into the house. Mom had no other life except for her job. No wonder she was sick. I'd just have to keep a closer eye on her, maybe take turns getting up in the night to check on Grandpa.

"Okay, Mark. I'm not going to argue with you."

"Good."

Dad got up and came to the sink where I was standing. He rinsed his cup and set it in the rack. "It sure is good to see you again, son."

"I've been right here all the time," I said. But I really didn't feel like fighting with him. Maybe it was a good sign that Mom felt she could call and talk to him. They had been married once, after all.

"I've been so busy with the new job, you just wouldn't believe it," Dad said. "I'm on the road a lot now, but once I've got this thing nailed down, you and I are going to have to get to know each other all over again."

Same old line. "Sure, Dad," I said.

"Your mother called me because she needed another opinion. The two of you are too close to the problem. She wants us to have a look at some of the places that are available for your grandfather. These homes usually have waiting lists, so we have to act soon."

The door opened and Mrs. Fuller helped Grandpa back inside. "Richard," said Grandpa again, when he saw Dad.

"That's right, Luigi. You remembered."

It was funny the way my grandfather knew Dad. He probably hadn't seen him in years, possibly since Grandma's funeral, and hadn't had a good word to say about him since he took off. It was like those old pictures of all his relatives he had in his room. He knew every one of them. But some days, he didn't know his own daughter or grandson.

Mom slept the entire weekend. Dad hung around to help me with Grandpa, although he sure had a lot to learn about looking after people. But Grandpa really seemed to like having him around.

On Sunday afternoon, Dad took Grandpa and me for a ride in his car. "Man, this place hasn't changed in 20 years," observed Dad, looking from side to side at the row of shops on the main street. "Even smells the same."

"I never noticed the smell."

"How could you miss it? It's the most distinctive thing about the place. I'm just sorry you and Giovanna have to live here."

"Don't be. Grandpa needed us."

"You're a good kid, Mark. Just like your mother, always making the best of things." That shows you how much he knew.

"No, really, Dad. I thought I'd hate it, but it's not so bad."

"And I guess it wouldn't bother your mother. This is where she grew up. And that school? I can't believe it's still here." Dad shook his head.

He had to concentrate in order to stay out of the streetcar tracks. We stopped at a park outside the city limits. "I thought your grandpa would like to breathe some clean air," Dad said. "Think he'd like to walk a bit?"

Grandpa swung his legs around so that they were sticking out of the car door, but he resisted getting up.

"It's okay, Dad. Just let him sit there like that. He doesn't know this place."

Dad and I went and sat down on the warm grass on a bank where we could keep an eye on the car, our legs outstretched in front of us.

"So, how's it going?" Dad asked. "Any girlfriends?"

I pulled up a blade of long grass and bit the sweet, white end off it. "Nope," I said.

"Not interested in girls yet?"

"No one special. I did have a girlfriend back at the other place. Well, not actually a girlfriend. Just someone I liked a lot. But she's going with Travis Devries now anyway."

It was always like this with Dad. I'd start off being defensive, resenting the way he criticized our life, Mom's and mine. And then I'd end up telling him all my secrets.

"Did I ever meet Travis?"

I looked him squarely in the eye. "You never visited us there, Dad." When he was quiet for a few minutes, I asked. "What about you? No girlfriends?" There had been someone once, when I went to spend a weekend with him. Someone named Jenny, I think.

"No one special. My work makes it pretty hard for any woman. I'm not home much."

I had to ask it. "You think there'd ever be a chance you and Mom could work things out and get back together again?"

"I'm afraid not, son. Too much water under the bridge for that. You're not still hoping for that, are you?"

"You did say you still cared about her."

"Of course I care. I'll always care. But we've both made new lives for ourselves now." He frowned, watching Grandpa in the car. "Does he always do that?" he asked.

"Do what?"

"Rock back and forth like that."

"Sometimes."

"Can't you make him stop?"

"Why? Is it bothering you?"

"It's driving me crazy."

"The only way you can make him stop something is to distract him. Give him something else to do."

"Oh. Do you think he has to go to the bathroom?"

"I don't think so. But maybe we'd better be getting back anyway."

When we got home, Mom was downstairs for the first time in three days. We'd brought fried chicken for supper and she joined us for the meal, looking drained but insisting she was much better.

"Thanks, Richard, for staying," Mom said, when we went to the door later to see Dad off. "It was good of you to come."

"I'll be in town till next Wednesday," Dad said. "We can check those places out any evening."

"Don't worry about it. You've helped me come to a decision. Mark and I can take it from here."

Dad nodded. "You sure there isn't anything you two need?" He was jiggling his car keys, one foot on the bottom step.

"We're fine," said Mom, her arm around my shoulders. We presented a united front, but I was supporting her weight.

"What about you, Mark? Couldn't you use a little extra cash?"

I straightened up. This was the first time I'd ever heard this offer. "As a matter of fact, I could."

"Mark!" Mom protested.

"Well, it's true, Mom. I need nine dollars and some spending money for my school trip. Mr. Hoskins put the money in for me, but I still have to pay him back."

85

Dad immediately pulled his wallet out of his back pocket. Maybe nine dollars was a small price to pay for getting off the hook so easily.

CHAPTER 6

I had just pulled my head out of the fridge and was taking a huge bite out of one of Mrs. Fuller's taffy tarts when I saw the note. It was attached to the fridge door by one of the cow magnets.

"Mark. Man at newspaper office called. Wants to talk to you. Mrs. F."

Since I'd come in from school, we'd both been trying to get Grandpa settled down, and she had forgotten to tell me Bernie had called.

Grandpa had had a bad day. He'd been pacing restlessly all afternoon and wringing his hands. Nothing Mrs. Fuller had tried seemed to relieve his agitation.

"He couldn't tell me what was bothering him, poor soul," she said. "I thought bringing him the seed catalogue this morning might cheer him up. You know, seeing all those wonderful vegetables and plants? He does seem better now that you're here."

Sometimes there was no way of knowing what would cause Grandpa to become upset. He would start pacing through the house, moaning, as if he were looking for someone. Fussing just made him worse. All we could do was talk to him gently and keep calm ourselves. This time it seemed to quiet him when Mrs. Fuller and I sat down in rocking chairs beside his in the sunroom and looked out at the street, as if it were something we all did together every day of our lives. After a while he stopped rocking and went over to the daybed. Lying down on it, he curled up on his side like a child. I went in to the telephone to call Bernie.

"Can you drop by the office?" Bernie asked. "I'd like to talk something over with you. Fairly important."

"Can't you tell me what it is over the telephone?" I wondered.

"I'll wait for you," said Bernie and promptly hung up.

Mrs. Fuller came through to the kitchen. "He's resting now," she whispered, putting a finger to her lips.

I told her I'd only be gone a few minutes. I'd go out the back way.

"That's fine, Mark," she said. "Would you have time to pick up those things on your mother's list? She left the money for them on the fridge."

The girl was just putting the cover on the computer when I got there. "How're you doing?" I asked.

"So-so," she said, with her usual shrug.

"So, Bernie. Here I am."

"Right." He got his rumpled jacket off a coat rack, before coming to the counter to talk to me. "I was wondering if you and that other kid who wanted the job might be able to handle it together."

"Handle what?"

"Your old job. Delivering flyers."

"Oh. What other kid?"

"You know. The one who came in right behind you, the day you came to see about the job. The one you say's been giving you the hard time."

"Randy Smits? No way!"

"Why not? Co-operation, Mark. It might work if you tried it."

"You don't know Randy Smits. He doesn't co-operate with anybody."

"So what's the matter with him?"

"I told you how he wouldn't let me deliver the ads on his street, right? He wrecked my bike. I've got no transportation now anyhow."

"Well, I still haven't found anyone to replace you, kid. Stacey and I tried delivering the flyers ourselves last week."

"You did? We didn't get any at our house."

"There. What did I tell you, Stace?"

The girl shrugged helplessly.

"Look," Bernie continued. "If two kids worked together, they could do it. If they didn't object to sharing the profits."

"It's not that," I insisted. "I probably can't look after the whole route anyway. I have to be home every day by four. But I'd share the route with anyone except Randy."

"Well, Randy was the one who applied for the job, so it's only fair. You'd both make some money and the job would get done quicker."

"I don't know, Bernie," I hesitated. I hadn't expected anything like this.

"You need money, don't you? What kid doesn't."

"Sure, but..."

"How'd it be if I paid to have that bike of yours fixed?"

"You weren't the one who wrecked it."

"Of course not. But I'd like to do this for you. And for me. Why don't you just try it, see if you can't share the job with this archenemy of yours."

"He'll kill me if I put a foot on his street. Let's put it this way, Bernie. We hate each other's guts."

"Just suggest it to him, kid. Okay? I know it

won't be easy. But look at it as a challenge. It could solve everyone's problem."

"I don't have a problem. If I just stay out of Randy Smits' way."

"No. But you don't have a job either."

"We don't even talk, Randy and me." I seemed to be whining.

"So try the telephone. That always makes things easier. And Mark," he said, as he came around the counter to where Stacey was waiting by the door. "Bring me that bike in the morning. You'll be needing it next week."

I didn't say no, but I was going to have to think about this.

* * *

I was just coming in the front door of the house with the groceries when Mrs. Fuller came hurrying in the back. "Mark, come quickly! Your grandfather's fallen!" All thoughts of Bernie's suggestion flew from my mind.

I dropped the plastic shopping bag in the kitchen, the cans of soup rolling off the table and onto the floor. Grandpa was outside, lying at the foot of the back steps, a small, gray heap, crying loudly.

"I was just going in to call the ambulance," said

Mrs. Fuller, as we hurried down to him. "I'm afraid he's really hurt bad. I couldn't get him up."

"Grandpa? Grandpa?" I knelt beside him and tried to take his flailing arms to calm him. "It's okay, Grandpa. We'll get you some help."

The high pitched wailing continued and I scrambled back up the steps on all fours. "I'll call the ambulance," I shouted. "You stay with him."

The emergency numbers were taped to the wall right next to the phone, but I was shaking so badly I had to hang up and redial twice. Then I went back outside and joined Mrs. Fuller on the ground beside my terrified grandfather.

That was the way the ambulance attendants found us. "Looks like his hip," one of them said, as they slid the stretcher bearing Grandpa on it into the back of the ambulance. "Who's coming with him?"

"You go with Luigi, Markie," urged Mrs. Savalas who, along with several other neighbours, had come over to our back yard, summoned by Grandpa's loud cries of pain. She gave me a little shove. "I'll stay with the lady here and we'll call Giovanna."

I climbed into the back of the ambulance and, with sirens wailing, we swept away from the curb, leaving the little crowd with worried faces standing there.

It was his hip. The fall on the steps had shattered the bone. "Not good, especially for someone his age," said Mom, echoing the doctor's words. We sat together in the waiting room next to the nurses' station, hours later. The doctor had told us they were going to have to put a pin in Grandpa's broken hip. His recovery could be a slow one, although this operation was one they performed every day.

"He was really upset today, Mom," I remembered to tell her. "Mrs. Fuller had a hard time with him."

"I know. I talked to her on the phone." She smoothed the hair back off my forehead. "You'd better go on home now, Mark. I'll call a taxi for you."

"No way. I'm waiting here with you."

"No, Mark. Grandpa will be okay now that the sedative has taken effect. He'll sleep. They're finding a place for me, so that I can stay the night."

"But you just got over being sick yourself."

"I'll be fine. Mrs. Fuller said she'd stay at the house for the night."

"What if you need me?"

"Then I'll know right where to find you. And don't worry. This is the best possible place for your grandfather right now. You know that's true."

Word travels fast in our neighbourhood. Even

Mr. Hoskins had heard about Grandpa's accident by the time I got to school the next day. "You'll keep me posted on his condition, won't you, Mark?"

Mom had called before I left in the morning, to say the orthopedic surgeon was operating on Grandpa's hip, and that, if all went well, they'd have him up and using a walker in no time. That made me feel much better.

With all the excitement, I wasn't ready to approach Randy with the idea of job sharing with me yet. I knew I was going to have to make a decision soon, though. Bernie had told me to bring my bike down to him the next day. Maybe his idea of asking Randy over the telephone was the best one. At least, he wouldn't be able to reach me physically that way.

"He's not going to go for it," Nick predicted gloomily, as we walked home from school that afternoon. At least, I walked. He rode his bike in little teetery circles around me.

"Bernie says I've got to give him the chance. But if Randy doesn't go for it, maybe someone else will. Maybe even you."

"Can't. I've got to look after Jessie. You want to come up to the house for a while?"

I didn't have any reason to hurry home this afternoon. Mrs. Fuller was on holiday until Grandpa came home. Suddenly I felt as if I'd sprouted wings. I was free! Nobody needed me!

Jessie was sitting on the front step, hugging a large cat and waiting for her brother. "Mom said I couldn't ever go in the house till you got here, Nickie. What took you so long?"

"You let that cat go," said Nick, ignoring the question, as he wheeled his bike up the walk. "You know you aren't supposed to have any more cats around here."

"Mr. Lo has puppies, Nickie," the little girl said. She got up, still clutching the orange cat. "You want to see them? The gate's locked, but Mr. Lo said sometime I could pick one up. Maybe tomorrow."

We went around to the side of the house and looked over the fence into the neighbour's yard. The Lo's big yellow dog was lying on her side, half under the back porch, and a wiggling, squirming mass of black and yellow puppies pressed their heads against her belly.

"You better not try picking up any of those pups till that mother dog lets you," said Nick, lifting his little sister off the fence and setting her down firmly. Her tee shirt was grubby from the schoolyard and her brown hair had come out of her stubby braids.

"I know, Nickie," Jessie said and ran to catch the cat again, which had gone to hide under the bushes.

I wished I could get a closer look at the puppies myself. I hadn't forgotten Mom's offer of a dog.

Nick had to take Jessie inside, so I went and helped them eat bread and peanut butter before I went home.

Nick had said the Los always gave their puppies away when they were about six weeks old. At that price, even I could afford one. And if I did take Bernie up on his job sharing idea, I could afford to buy food for a dog.

I was just turning up my street when I saw, coming towards me, Randy Smits walking with Rhonda. I pretended not to see them and crossed to the other side as coolly as possible, even paused for a moment as though I had an errand at the first house and was thinking about going up to the door.

"Hey, Rogers!" Randy yelled. "My ma wants to know how come you don't deliver any of those cheap papers to our house anymore. We not good enough for you or something?"

It was the first time he'd spoken to me in weeks. Probably wanted to look good for Rhonda. Deliberately, I crossed back to their side of the street. Well, here was my chance. And with Rhonda here, he wouldn't push me around, would he?

"I think you know why you aren't getting

your papers," I said bravely.

"No. Tell me," Randy said, giving Rhonda a smirk.

I pretended to start around them and carry on my way home. "But you don't have to worry about me anymore," I said, as I stepped down into the street to pass them. "I'm not delivering flyers anywhere now."

"How come?"

"I got fired. The guy at the newspaper office figures no kid could do it quick enough."

"Not you anyways, Rogers."

"He says two guys could do it, though."

"So?"

"Even wonders if you'd like to take part of the route."

"Yeah? Me and who else?"

"Me." I took advantage of his surprise to continue. "Otherwise, neither one of us gets the job and he gives it to someone with a car."

"That'll be me in a couple of years," Randy grinned, shoving the tips of his fingers into the back pockets of his jeans. "I can drive already. Just have to wait till I turn 16."

"Say, Mark," Rhonda piped up. "I was sorry to hear about your grandfather's accident. Is he going to be okay? That speech you gave about him was really good."

"Well, yours was the best. It deserved to win."

She nodded. "So, Randy. What do you say? You going to take on this job with Mark or not?"

"I could do the whole thing with one hand tied behind my back," he bragged.

"Okay, let's see you," she dared and, twisting his arm playfully behind him, she started to walk him on tiptoes up the street away from me.

"Okay, okay! I give up. Hey, wait a sec, Rogers. You tell that guy we'll take his job."

"Okay, if you say so," I replied evenly, although the relief I felt was making me feel I'd burst any minute.

Wow! This had been much easier than I'd expected. I watched them turn the corner. Then I ran the rest of the way home and dragged my battered bike out of the shed.

CHAPTER 7

On Saturday, Mom and I had company. There's nothing unusual about that; we had people dropping by all the time now to ask how Grandpa was or to bring us dishes of food. Food seemed to be the way the people in the East End expressed their concern. But I certainly never expected to find Mr. Hoskins standing on our front step when I answered the door.

He was returning the typewritten copy of my speech. "I thought you or your mother might like to keep this," he explained.

I'm sure I must have had a blank look on my face. Even though I knew he and Mom knew each other from the olden days, a kid doesn't expect his Grade Eight teacher to show up at his place on a Saturday. I only hoped none of the kids from school had seen him come here.

"Aren't you going to invite our guest in?" Mom

asked, coming up behind me and reminding me of my manners.

"Hello, Giovanna," said Mr. Hoskins.

"Hello, Art," said Mom. She stepped aside so he could enter. "I've just made some iced tea. Come out the back and join me." Was he the reason I'd had to try to repair the two old lawn chairs before I could take off for Nick's?

Mr. Hoskins stayed for iced tea and later drove Mom to the hospital to see her father. I guess he was just being considerate, like everyone else in the neighbourhood had been. Besides the food, which meant Mom and I hadn't had to cook a meal in over two weeks, we had so many offers of rides to the hospital that she drew up a roster of who was taking her on which days.

I had stopped going every day to see Grandpa after the first week. Now I just went on weekends. He didn't know who I was anyway.

Being in the hospital made Grandpa more confused than ever. Mom had brought him all his family pictures and would sit beside him telling him who they all were. It didn't seem to help. He just picked at the blankets with anxious fingers and stared into space.

"What are we going to do, Mom?" I hated to see him like that. "He's so unhappy."

But Mom didn't know either. "They're doing all they can," she said. The nurses tried to assure us that he was as comfortable as could be expected.

From the very first day in hospital, Grandpa had stopped trying to speak and suddenly he stopped eating too. Mom tried feeding him herself, thinking it would remind him of when he was home, but he refused even to open his mouth. Day after day, she persevered, but it did no good.

"Couldn't we take him some of his favourite food?" I asked. But he hadn't had any favourites for a long time. Even before the accident, everything had had to be soft and mushy or in very small pieces because he had forgotten how to chew properly.

When I went with Mom on Sunday to see him, we stopped first at the store across from the hospital and bought a small cup of ice cream for Grandpa as a treat. When we got to his room, we saw he was not going to be able to eat it. Now there were plastic tubes running in and out of him. Mom gave the ice cream to the nurse, before it melted completely.

At home, it was easier to forget how bad it was in the hospital and we started getting things ready for Grandpa's return. "He'll feel better when he's back among familiar things," Mom said. She had housecleaned his room and washed and ironed the curtains and the cushion covers on the daybed and his favourite chair.

One Saturday, I even cleaned the rust off some of his tools in the shed, although he hadn't bothered to go out there in weeks. I promised myself that when he got home I'd go and sit there in the little shed and just let him putter until he got tired of it.

A long time ago, Grandpa had traced the shapes of the tools on the wall where each one belonged. One by one, I placed them back on the hooks where he had left them.

A week later, my Grandpa died.

I heard the phone ring in the night, heard Mom get up and go down to it. I heard her open the gate she had absentmindedly shut when she went up to bed. We hadn't needed to keep Grandpa off the stairs for a while.

"He's gone, Mark," she said, standing quietly in the open doorway of my room.

"Who's gone?"

"Your grandfather. He died a few minutes ago."

"Oh," I said. "That's okay, Mom."

She started to leave. I sat up suddenly then, thinking what a stupid thing I'd just said.

"Are you all right, Mom?" I called. The door to her room closed softly. She needed to be alone, I guess. I wondered if she'd be crying, and if I should go and comfort her like she used to comfort me when I was little. I didn't hear anything. It felt to me as if Grandpa had died a long time ago. Maybe even when my Grandma had.

* * *

Grandpa's funeral was on the day I was supposed to leave for Ottawa on our school trip. I saw the yellow school bus go by the top of the street when I opened the door to Mrs. Savalas and another tray of sandwiches. The graduating class was getting away right on time.

Mr. Hoskins and the kids in homeroom sent a bouquet of flowers to the house for Mom. "Flowers for the living," she said, setting the arrangement on the table under the window and turning it till it suited her.

Everyone in the neighbourhood seemed to turn out for the funeral. Even, to my surprise, Nick.

"Why didn't you go on the trip?" I asked, when I caught up with him at the door of the church. He was wearing his brother's suit which his mother had shortened for graduation.

"Naw," he said. "It wouldn't be right. Not when your best friend's grandfather dies."

Afterwards, the little house was overflowing with people and food. "Ah, I just wish Luigi could be here," said one of Grandpa's old friends. The rest of them nodded and muttered in agreement. "That Luigi, he sure loved a party." Now that was the Grandpa I remembered.

Mom had been unable to reach Dad to tell him the news. We knew he'd want to be at the funeral. All we could do was leave a message on his answering machine.

Finally, all the neighbours left and Mom and I sat on the back steps together in the late afternoon sunshine. Nick had had to hurry home to be with Jessie.

What little grass there had been in my grandfather's back yard was now completely flattened by so many pairs of feet. Mr. Singh had left his shiny suit coat hanging on the fence when he'd helped to carry the kitchen chairs back inside for us.

Mom had taken her shoes off and I'd gone to hang up my good shirt. It had been a long day. She put an arm around my shoulders and leaned her head against mine. "Grandpa would have been so sorry you missed your trip, Mark," she said.

I knew he would have been. I was glad I'd saved his silver dollars, though. They had been the last things my grandfather had given me. Or so I thought.

"It's just the two of us now," Mom said.

I nodded. For the past month, it had been

just the two of us. But after weeks and weeks of looking after Grandpa, it felt strange for him to be gone. I still kept listening for him, and every time I passed his room I looked in, expecting to see him sitting there, staring at the wall.

"So, now what?" Mom smoothed her black dress down over her knees, leaned her arms on them and smiled over her shoulder at me. "Do we stay here, Mark? Or move on?"

I hadn't ever figured we'd have to move on. But of course, our reason for coming here was gone now. "Can we stay here?"

"We certainly can. If you want to. I haven't had a chance to tell you today, but Grandpa left the house to me."

"All right! We stay!" A house of our own. "If it's okay with you, Mom. You're the one with the long ride to work everyday."

"It's not so bad. You wouldn't mind staying here? This old neighbourhood doesn't bother you?"

"Nope. This is home now. Besides, you promised me a dog. Remember?" I hoped it wasn't too soon to bring the subject up again.

"You're right. I did, didn't I. You want to take a look at those puppies you were telling me about?"

"You mean right now? Is it okay?"

"Can't see why not. Did I ever tell you about

the time your grandfather showed up here with a dog? Worst looking mutt you ever saw. Your grandmother was furious. At least, she pretended to be. Tell you what, you take Mr. Singh back over his jacket and I'll meet you out front."

Nick saw us at his next door neighbour's and came over to help me choose a puppy. Jessie was already there, sitting on the trampled ground, cradling a fat black pup on her lap.

"She thinks these dogs belong to her," Nick complained. "She can't have one."

"Nothing wrong with being an animal lover," said Mom.

"Take this one, Mark," Jessie offered, handing me the puppy she'd been holding. That one had been my choice too. It nestled its warm head into my neck, as if it knew me already.

"Oh, my gosh, she's got the saddest eyes," cried Mom. "She's a real heart-breaker. You sure it's okay to take her, Jessie? You have to promise to come and visit her whenever you can." The little girl's face lit up like a Christmas tree.

"You'll never get rid of her now," Nick grumbled.

The pup slept with me the first night because she whimpered with loneliness. Having her with me made me feel better, too.

It didn't take the three of us long to get used to living with each other. We called her Chelsea II, which I suppose wasn't very original. Her legs were still too short to get up and down the stairs to my bedroom by herself, so she decided the mat at the foot of the stairs would be her special place. With school out in another week, I'd have the whole summer to train her.

* * *

On the last morning of school, Randy Smits caught up with Nick and me as we cycled through the warm June streets together. "Say, Rogers," Randy called, peddling past, his arms crossed and his hands in his armpits. "My ma wants to know how come she didn't get her flyer yesterday."

"That's your route, Smits," I yelled back.

"Just kidding," he said, leaning again to the handlebars. "She got it. And on time for a change, too!"

Peggy Dymond Leavey was born in Toronto, but as her father was in the Canadian military forces during the war years, she received her education in nine different schools between Winnipeg, Manitoba and Fort Chambly, Quebec. She now lives in the Trenton area of Ontario, where she has raised three children. Besides her work as a librarian, she has published many books on local history and done freelance writing for adults and children.